SO-DOP-879

THE ADVENTURES OF

PRINCE ALBERT

and

THE ROYAL DINOSAURS

Albert stood on his hind legs and
performed the Dinny Hop.

THE ADVENTURES OF PRINCE ALBERT

and
THE ROYAL DINOSAURS

By Frank A. Manson

Illustrated by Joan Henley

VANDAMERE PRESS
a division of AB Associates

Published by
Vandamere Press
A division of AB Associates
P. O. Box 5243
Arlington, Virginia
22205

ISBN 0-918339-17-0
Library of Congress Card Number 90-070845

Manufactured in the United States of America. This book is typeset in ITC Benguiat and Century Old Style. Book design, typography, and production by AAH, Seven Fountains, VA 22652

To my wife, Orie Lee, our children and grandchildren.

Acknowledgements

Grateful thanks are due my grandson, Albert Karig Manson, Raleigh, N.C., a serious student of dinosaurs. We had frequent discussions. His drawings included such details as shapes, sizes, horns, teeth, claws and food preferences. Albert gave me an insight into the living habits of dozens of dinosaurs.

In this book Karig is King of the Brontosauruses. His name comes from my friend, the late Walter Karig, who wrote the early volumes of Nancy Drew using the pen name Carolyn Keene. I was privileged to write several books with him.

The illustrator, Joan Henley, a noted wildlife artist from Roanoke, Va., carefully studied the manuscript. She researched each dinosaur before she painted it. Her art gave each royal dinosaur a distinctive personality.

Smithsonian's paleontologist, Dr. Ian Macintyre, provided needed advice during the writing of the manuscript. Delores Jackson, Fort Washington, Md. and Mary Beth Straight, Annapolis, Md., helped with the manuscript as did the professional touches of book experts, Ann and Stephen Hunter working from their mountain studio in Seven Fountains, Va. Shirley Schulz and L.J. Fox, both of Northern Virginia, helped bring the author and publisher together.

The publisher, Art Brown and his editor, Pat Berger, gave the royal dinosaurs their final polish. To all the above I am most appreciative.

Frank A. Manson

Table of Contents

Chapter 1

The Royal Dinosaurs

Deep in Carolina's blue-green Mesozoic swamps, a large group of dinosaurs lived in a magical kingdom. Despite their many sizes, shapes, and colors, the dinosaurs had one unusual thing in common. They had learned to talk!

The mystical kingdom was ruled by a pair of easy-going and gentle Brontosauruses. They had long necks, long tails, barrel-shaped bodies and legs the size of old tree trunks. They lived on plants, tree leaves and underwater grasses. The ruler's names were King Karig and Queen Violet.

Each dinosaur had its own idea of how King Karig and Queen Violet came to be rulers of the kingdom. Smaller dinosaurs, such as the Ankylosauruses with the bony armored shells on their backs, said the Brontosauruses kept the crown because they were so strong and tall. They noted that any member of the royal family could lift its head above the jungle and look down on most tree tops and on all the other creatures below. Small dinosaurs also noted the royal family's footsteps shook the earth when they approached. The Brontosauruses looked like moving mountains of muscle, flesh and bones.

Other dinosaurs had a different idea. They thought the royal couple got their power from a magical member of the kingdom, Judge Owl.

Judge Owl had arrived as a mystery guest in the dinosaur

kingdom. No one knew where he came from, and the Judge was not about to tell. The truth was that in another time and place an evil witch had chased him from her castle because he tried to teach her that good was better than evil. The witch's loss proved to be the king's gain.

Judge Owl was a wise old bird. He taught the dinosaurs to speak. In spite of their plum-sized brains the Judge had tried, with some success, to teach them to think. With the least bit of excitement, though, the dinosaurs got confused. Judge Owl continued to teach new words and numbers but the dinosaurs were slow learners.

Others thought the Brontosauruses had been selected to rule because they were calm. Also, a whipping blow from their powerful tails would keep ordinary dinosaurs in line.

King Karig and Queen Violet lived with their family in a palatial cave near the swamps. Judge Owl had selected the cave for the royal family because it was protected. They were the only dinosaurs who lived in such a splendid manner.

Above the cave's opening stood a large clump of tropical ferns and one coconut palm where Judge Owl perched. The cave was filled with tall caverns whose walls were made of large flat rocks. Overhead, water dripped down the walls making designs that fascinated members of the royal family and their guests. Long, shining stalactites hung from the cave's ceiling. These were covered by specks of gold and silver which dripped on the floor. Gold dust sometimes stuck to the royal family's feet making their footprints easy to spot along dinosaur trails.

King Karig and Queen Violet spent much of their time inside their palace cave. Besides eating enormous amounts of food, the King spent his spare time trying to contact other dinosaur kingdoms. His aim was to shorten wars and lengthen periods of peace. Meanwhile, Queen Violet studied insects, especially fireflies, because they might provide a source of light for the entire dinosaur world.

Queen Violet's other interest centered on the health of her subjects. She held classes for young plant-eating dinosaurs inside the palace. She taught them which plants to eat if they wanted to grow strong, and which plants, if eaten, would cause stomachaches. Her daughter, Princess Elizabeth worked to improve the royal wardrobe by designing new types of crowns, sashes, clasps, royal cloaks and leg warmers. The younger son, Prince Andrew, searched for large coconuts, of which we will learn more later.

Most of the kingdom's day-to-day operations were carried out by Crown Prince Albert. His parents had given him full authority for the many royal duties. They knew such training would help him become a strong king. When he wasn't training to be King, Prince Albert practiced dinosaur sports. His favorite sport was a game called *Koo Koo Nut*, the oldest form of soccer. Albert frequently practiced his turns, his change of direction, his twists and how to stand on his hind legs. He loved another dinosaur sport called mudsliding which sometimes brought sliders to the edge of danger. Albert considered mudsliding high adventure.

Prince Albert could count on Judge Owl to help in running an orderly kingdom. Fights with the meat eaters, mostly Allosauruses, did cause problems for the kingdom. One swish of Albert's tail however, sent the greedy Allosauruses scampering for the bushes. Albert also had frequent trouble with plant eaters called Triceratops, each with three horns on his nose. Dangerous Dan, leader of the Triceratops, usually helped Albert settle their disputes.

Prince Albert's favorite group of dinosaurs was the Stegosauruses with their shiny big plates growing from their backbones and tails. He had such confidence in the Stegosauruses he persuaded his father to hire four of them as guards for the palace. Captain Stego, their leader, had proven his loyalty to the crown on a number of occasions. Unfortunately, Captain Stego had more brawn and bravery than he had brains.

Chapter 2

The Dinosaurs Prepare to Play *Koo Koo Nut*

When one or more dinosaurs decided it was time for a game they would lift their noses toward the sky and make a howling sound. They opened their mouths wide and howled out the syllables "koooo koooo nut, koooo koooo nut." These sounds would pass from one dinosaur to another until eventually as many as one hundred animals would know the game was about to begin. Hearing the "koooo koooo nut" sound was enough to attract dozens of dinosaurs: the meat eaters, the plant eaters, those confined to the ground and those able to fly.

One day a big-tailed Brontosaurus dinosaur known in the region by the name of Prince Albert heard a soft howl very near him. Prince Albert knew from the softness of the howl it was his younger brother, Prince Andrew, calling.

Being a young dinosaur, Prince Andrew's howl sounded soft and clear. "Koooo koooo nut, koooo koooo nut," howled the youngster. Prince Albert lifted his large head high in the air and cocked an ear. "Yes, it was Andrew," thought Albert. No other dinosaur sounded like his younger brother. Grazing in tall grasses nearby, Princess Elizabeth galloped over to Albert.

"Did you hear Andrew?"

"Yes," Albert said, "but I was hoping to finish the leaves from this magnolia tree before responding." Albert chewed the magnolia leaves feverishly. He also chewed the Magnolia's large white blossoms. His mouth drew in leaves like a vacuum cleaner. His tongue served as a magnet.

"Do you wish me to reply?" Elizabeth asked politely. She knew *Koo Koo Nut* was Albert's game. He was one of the best players in the Carolina Blue Swamp country. In fact Albert's reputation was so widespread that some of the dinosaurs called Prince Albert the "big blue devil." Albert didn't mind being called a blue devil because he knew it was a sign of respect. Besides, his skin was blue-gray and so were his eyes.

Albert knew Andrew had found a large coconut, probably as large as his foot. He had taught Andrew to call out only when he had found a truly large one.

"Hold your spot," Albert shouted as soon as he had swallowed his last mouthful of magnolia blossoms and large green leaves. "Hold your spot, Andrew. Elizabeth and I will pass the word to other dinosaurs downwind." Dinosaurs appreciated stronger winds because they could hear longer distances. With a strong wind they could be heard two or three miles.

As Albert and Elizabeth made their way through the jungle and vines, pushing most of them flat under their huge stomachs, once more they heard Andrew's soft howl, "koooo koooo nut."

"Hold the spot, Andrew," shouted Albert. "We hear you. We hear you." Meanwhile Elizabeth was helping Albert pass the word to all the dinosaurs within hearing distance. "Koooo koooo nut, koooo koooo nut," they repeated. And as other dinosaurs heard Albert and Elizabeth they lifted their heads skyward above the treetops to repeat what they had heard.

"It's too bad the meat eaters must hear and will most likely join us," said Albert.

"That's why I prefer to watch the game and not play," said Elizabeth. "Those meat eaters take all the fun out of it." "But a dinosaur has to do what a dinosaur has to do," snorted Albert, his eyes growing large and his nostrils flaring.

Elizabeth could see her brother, Prince Albert, already

Albert chewed the magnolia leaves feverishly.

ng his mind for the game. Albert was not afraid of the eaters. One whack of his powerful tail would send most dinosaurs reeling in a daze.

"If none of the meat eaters come," said Elizabeth, "I will play."

"We'll see which dinosaurs show up," said Albert as he strolled over to Andrew and gave him a friendly neck rub for finding such a beautiful coconut.

Andrew closed his eyes when Albert gave him the friendly rub. He appreciated the attention of his family.

The game of *Koo Koo Nut* usually required three days: one day for assembly and preparing the field, one day for practice and one day for playing the game.

Each day was filled with excitement and surprises. The dinosaurs enjoyed large meetings. It gave them a chance to exchange experiences, tell each other where they had travelled and what they had seen plus discover all the news about the hatching of baby dinosaurs. Albert's main interest was news about other Brontosauruses. "One problem we have," Albert told Elizabeth, "is too few plant eaters and too many meat eaters." Elizabeth agreed. The game of *Koo Koo Nut* would be safer and more fun if only the Brontosauruses played.

Albert and Elizabeth had barely begun to clear trees from the playing field when three unexpected Brontosauruses arrived from a place called Merry Land.

"Welcome to Blue Swamp country," said Albert to the three new arrivals.

"I'm Baron Von Zack," said the largest of the new arrivals, "And this is my sister, Lady May, and my cousin, Lady Lynne. We come from the Gunn clan. We represent a royal line."

"Did your feet get cold when you walked across the ice?" Elizabeth asked, looking at the two rather small dinosaurs, Lady May and Lady Lynne. Their delicate skin did not seem sufficiently thick or tough to deal with harsh cold weather.

"No, no," said Baron Von Zack. "We walked on the sand down the coast from Merry Land. We have come to play *Koo Koo Nut*."

"We are expecting meat eaters," said Albert. "And we can't trust the meat eaters. Sometimes when the game gets rough, those meat eaters will take a bite from your neck or leg."

Zack's eyes widened. His nostrils flared. "I'll bang them with my tail," said Zack.

"Exactly correct," said Albert. "You are a strong Brontosaurus. You are part of my royal clan, but we dare not risk the smaller ones."

"Albert is right," said Elizabeth. "I don't intend to play if the meat eaters come."

"I'm positive the meat eaters will come," said Albert.

"Let them come," said Zack, "and we'll give them a good banging."

Prince Albert admired Baron Von Zack's raw courage. It was apparent that he was ready for a rough game. Depending on what types of dinosaurs arrived for the game, it might be possible for Andrew, Elizabeth, May and Lynne to get a whack

"Welcome to Blue Swamp country,"
said Albert to the new arrivals.

or two at the coconut. Still, three of them were quite small, and Elizabeth did not want to play if meat eaters were in the game.

"Meat eaters might be safe in the early part of the game," Albert told the other five dinosaurs from his clan, "but when they get worked up and their blood runs hot they become dangerous. They bite before they think."

"They need a good banging," said Zack. "A few quick bangs from my tail will cool them down."

Albert's big jaw opened and a smile was visible from ear to ear. It was apparent that Zack had come to play hardball *Koo Koo Nut*. This pleased Albert for he wanted hardball players, especially against the meat eaters.

Before Albert had finished telling the new arrivals about clearing the playing fields and certain tips about the game, other dinosaurs began arriving. Shortly behind Baron Von Zack, Lady May and Lady Lynne came two more Brontosauruses from Merry Land. These two had followed Baron Von Zack along the sandy beaches.

"We welcome you," Albert said in greeting. "May I introduce five of my fellow clansmen. Two are from the Carolina Blue Swamp country and three from Merry Land." All the dinosaurs lowered their heads and smiled as they were formally introduced by title.

Albert had begun to think the game would be played by Brontosauruses exclusively when he heard some trees falling nearby.

"The trees are falling Albert," said Elizabeth.

"Even Baron Von Zack has cocked his ear," said Albert fully expecting to see some meat eaters. Instead, some horned Triceratops were arriving.

"Save your strength," thundered
Prince Albert in his deepest voice.

The tree would fall as if it had been
flattened by a hurricane . . .

Albert knew the Triceratops would try to make a bold entry into the game. What better way than knocking down a few trees near the game site?

"Save your strength," thundered Prince Albert in his deepest voice.

"If you want to knock down trees, help us clear the playing field."

"Show us the trees," honked Dangerous Dan, the senior member of the Triceratops clan.

Elizabeth, Andrew, May and Lynne were frightened when they looked at the sharp long horns protruding from the Triceratops' lower jaw and the sharp horn on his nose.

23

"If they are not meat eaters why do they have such sharp horns?" asked Elizabeth.

"For defense only," said Albert.

Then Albert selected the trees that needed removal. Dangerous Dan, or one of his mates, slowly placed the tree trunks between his horns and pushed. The trees fell as if flattened by a hurricane.

Albert moved close to Zack's ear to whisper some advice. "Our tails are stronger than the Triceratops'" he told Zack, who nodded in agreement.

"How do we deal with those long sharp horns?" asked one of the Merry Landers, Lady May. Lady Lynne's lower lip jutted out from fright. Those awful horns caused all the female Brontosauruses to squirm.

"Just bang their feet with your tail," said Albert, "and they'll back off."

"They look as if they need a good banging," said Zack.

"It all depends on how they play," said Albert. "If they keep their horns to themselves, we can have a nice clean game."

Next to arrive were one Tyrannosaurus rex and three Allosauruses, all with bad reputations, all meat eaters with long rows of sharp white teeth flashing in the sunlight.

"Looks as if we'll all have our tails full in this game," said Albert. All the Brontosauruses were in agreement.

The teeth of meat eaters offered more problems than the horns of Triceratops. Meat eaters had a terrible reputation among dinosaurs. When they grew tired, disgusted or hungry,

Next to arrive were one Tyrannosaurus rex
and three Allosauruses . . .

they tended to bite the nearest dinosaur. They preferred to bite plant eaters' necks and tails, but, in a pinch, they would bite a hunk from one of their own kind.

"Might as well call meat eaters cannibals," said Lady May.

"Do you suppose they brush their teeth with sand?" asked Lady Lynne, "Their teeth are so bright."

"Probably do use sand," said Baron Von Zack, taking a careful look at the five rows of sharp pointed teeth. "Sand would keep those points sharp."

"Don't worry about their teeth," said Prince Albert. "Remember a whack from our tails will spin them around."

Chapter 3

Final Touches to the Playing Field

As the dinosaurs continued to arrive at the playing field, Albert kept them busy clearing brush and trees, taking care to leave a clump of trees at each end of the field to serve as goals. To score a goal one side had to push, kick or whack the coconut into a clump of trees. It was similar to soccer. Because dinosaurs were slow and playing fields large, the first team to score usually won the game.

According to Dinosaur Regulations the playing field had to be 1 mile long, and 1/2 mile wide. By the time dinosaurs had gone up and down the field a few times, they became bone-tired. Time-out could be called by either captain when the team needed rest. But when one team called time-out, the other team considered it a sign of weakness.

While Albert and Zack supervised the tree and bush removal from the playing field, Elizabeth, Andrew, May and Lynne searched for another large coconut just in case the first one should get broken during the game.

The search for larger coconuts was the dinosaur version of hunting for Easter eggs. It was fun. During such times the big lizards became cozy. They sometimes shared their friendly feelings by calling each other their non-royal names.

Elizabeth told the Merry Landers they could call her "Gillian" in private, but in public her royal name was Princess

Elizabeth. May said she had another name, "Celeste." And Lynne admitted she had another name as well—Jennifer. Andrew said he had another name, Frank, but the dinosaurs had difficulty pronouncing the "F" because their lips were too thick.

"You'll just have to call me Andrew," said the young prince "and forget about FFFrank."

All the time, Albert was considering what he should do to give each team an equal opportunity to win. He certainly did not want to put all the meat eaters against the plant eaters. Such a game would turn into a war and someone might get hurt.

At last Albert came up with a solution, a strategy he thought would work. When choosing sides, he would split up the plant eaters and the meat eaters. Dangerous Dan, a Triceratops, would be captain on one team and Prince Albert would lead the other team.

Before announcing his plan, Prince Albert asked for a few hours to think by himself. All the dinosaurs agreed, but they told Albert not to think too long as they wanted to get on with the game. Actually Albert didn't think very long. Rather he rushed to his home place, a giant cave, where two wise old dinosaurs awaited the outcome of the game.

Albert galloped up to the cave's mouth and found his parents King Karig and Queen Violet watching dragonflies.

Albert explained to his parents that a number of dangerous dinosaurs had shown up, as well as some very young members of the Gunn clan from Merry Land. King Karig advised the young prince to go ahead with his plan, but with caution.

King Karig advised the young Prince
to go ahead with his plan.

If any player disobeyed the rules, he or she should be thrown out of the game by his own captain. Queen Violet told her son to make sure the young dinosaurs were kept out of danger.

As a final word of advice King Karig said, "Before you start the game, find out which Allosaurus is head of the clan."

"So far we have only one Tyrannosaurus," said Albert.

"Make him King of the Tyrants," said Karig. "He's probably getting old. The Allosauruses are smaller. They will obey his commands."

Albert felt comfortable with his plan now that he had the advice and blessings of King Karig and Queen Violet. After all they had taught him the game.

The first thing Albert did when he returned to the playing field was to hold a private conference with the one and only Tyrannosaurus rex.

"Will you guarantee the conduct of all the meat eaters?" asked Prince Albert, "for you are their King."

Proud to claim his title, the King of the Tyrants promised that all meat eaters would play fair and square. "No biting!" he said.

Albert held a conference with the
one and only Tyrannosaurus rex.

Chapter 4

The Game Begins

On the day of the game Prince Albert and Dangerous Dan made their selection of players. They flipped a coconut leaf to see who would select first. Each side could have ten players from such types as Brontosaurus, Allosaurus, Ankylosaurus, Trachodon, Stegosaurus, Triceratops, Tyrannosaurus rex and even one flying Pteranodon that had shown up.

Albert won the toss. His first choice was Baron Von Zack. Dangerous Dan chose Tyrannosaurus rex, King of the Tyrants. Then Albert offered Dangerous Dan a deal. He would give the flying Pteranodon to Dangerous Dan if the three small dinosaurs and his sister Elizabeth could play on his side.

The Pteranodon had added the new dimension of flight to the game. It was barely possible the players would see the coconut flying over their heads. But Albert thought the coconut was too heavy for the beak or the skinny legs and feet of the Pteranodon.

"Sure, you can have three small ones for one Pteranodon," said the Triceratops.

"How stupid of Albert," thought Dangerous Dan. "We can beat Prince Albert fair and square. We won't need to use our sharp horns. The flying Pteranodon will pick up the coconut with its feet and fly it across the goal. Three small dinosaurs from Merry Land will not help Albert's team. They are too young and weak."

Albert knew Dangerous Dan would make this mistake. Meanwhile, he drew up a secret plan with Baron Von Zack, Elizabeth, May, Andrew, and Lynne. Zack would position himself between Albert and the goal. When Albert got control of

Albert had drawn up a secret plan with
Baron Von Zack,
Elizabeth, May, Andrew, and Lynne.

the coconut, he would head for the goal. Zack would run ahead, moving sideways like a crab, thus clearing a path for Albert and the coconut. Albert would follow directly behind Zack's tail. Zack liked this plan. He knew he could shuffle sideways like a crab. Also, with his powerful tail, he could bang all the opponents off their feet. Before his opponents could get back on their feet, Albert would waddle down the field with his tail tightly curled around the coconut.

Albert still had one deep secret. If Dangerous Dan tried to use the Pteranodon to fly the coconut above their heads, his secret plan would be unfurled. On the playing field only Zack, Elizabeth, Andrew, May and Lynne knew the secret plan. Only they would be needed to do it.

The game began when Prince Albert howled "Koooo koooo nut" at which time Elizabeth pushed the coconut to the center of the field and quickly waddled away from the charge of Dangerous Dan and his sharp horns. The ground vibrated and trees shook as heavy-footed dinosaurs pounded the playing field.

During the game's first few hours, it was difficult to tell which side was winning. Dangerous Dan and his team had a strong battle plan. Their idea was to form a circle and roll the coconut with their snouts. The Triceratops' sharp horns made it tricky for the Brontosauruses to get into the circle without catching a sharp horn in their sides.

Prince Albert, a world-class player, had seen many *Koo Koo Nut* formations. He had broken up the famous "flying wedge," a play that sent offensive players down the field in an inverted "V." This formation looked like the point of a giant arrow. Albert had broken up the wedge during the African Red Sky finals by rolling his large body in front of the arrow's point.

In another championship game played on the opposite side of the earth called the Rising Sun tournament, Albert stopped an "I" formation. He became famous for a line across the head of the column.

Dangerous Dan's plan was simple and it confused the other team.

The game was opened when Prince Albert howled "Koooo koooo nut."

Dan's team simply encircled the player advancing the coconut. Players continued their circling routine as they edged themselves toward the goal..

Baron Von Zack's first reaction was to smack one side of the circle, caving it in with a good tail bashing. Prince Albert joined Zack causing a furious swishing of tails by both sides. Also, Albert's teammates pitched in with heavy pushing and shoving as well as kicking and pawing. All these moves, legal by dinosaur rules, did not stop Dan's whirling circle. Unless Albert's team could think of a quick answer, the game would soon be over and lost!

Being one of Albert's thinkers Princess Elizabeth trotted alongside her brother to help him with some high level planning.

"The best way to break a circle is draw a line through it," said the brainy Princess.

"How does one put a line through a circle of moving dinosaurs?" Albert asked impatiently. His breath was hot and steamy.

Baron Von Zack had an idea.

"I say pit horns against horns," said Zack. The Baron was suggesting that Prince Albert send his one and only Triceratops, known as Little Silver Bull, in a head-to-head clash with Dangerous Dan.

Albert thought for a moment, then nodded his head approvingly. "It makes sense," he said, "and while the Triceratops bang heads, you and I will crash-land through the gap."

"You've got it," said the Baron. "This is dinosaur chess, knight against knight, hard heads against hard heads."

Albert motioned for Little Silver Bull to join him in huddle and Albert put forth the daring plan. The plan pitted Little Silver Bull in a head-to-head clash with the feared and fearless Dangerous Dan. Albert explained that such a move, if it worked, would break the circle. It would create a gap through which Albert's team could penetrate. The plan was that Dan would become so occupied with his challenger, that he would forget to lead his team.

"It's my cup of coconut milk," said Little Silver Bull when he realized his opportunity to become a star.

"You should have asked sooner," said Little Silver Bull whose skin was a shade lighter than the other Triceratops. "I've been wanting a crack at Dan," he said. "He brags around that he's the top Triceratops. After he feels my horns, he'll know small dinosaurs have sharp horns."

"Go get him 'horns,'" roared Zack in a teasing voice and a tone so loud it could be heard by all the players. "Teach big Dan to dance."

Dangerous Dan had heard the Baron. He was not surprised to see Little Silver Bull charging toward him with his head lowered and his nose skimming the ground.

"I'll take care of that young whippersnapper," said Dangerous Dan to his teammates. "I'll puncture his balloon. He'll learn who's tops."

A strange quiet fell over the playing field as the two massive Triceratops, one slightly larger than the other, came pawing and snorting toward each other.

The Game Begins

Zack swished his tail quickly
and down went the Triceratops.

Then the air was shattered by the force of head-on blows. It was Bam! Bam! Crack! the two hit each other with full force. Both fell to their knees during the initial blows. It was head against horns, horns against head, and horns against horns as the sounds crashed in the air. The pride of each was on the line, since each thought himself better than the other. It sounded like the cracking of tree limbs in a thunderstorm..

Meanwhile, Albert and Zack did what they promised. They ran through the gap and did their stand-up and crash act toward the opposing dinosaurs. The sight of two Brontosauruses standing on their hind legs forced the opposing players to scatter. Even Tyrannosaurus rex slipped sideways to avoid the crash landings of the heavyweights. Clouds of dust lifted from the playing field, dust so thick the dinosaurs choked and gasped for breath, dust so dense the players could not tell friend from foe.

When the dust settled, all the fire had left the eyes of Dangerous Dan and Little Silver Bull. Both stood still in an apparent daze. Blood trickled from their numerous head wounds. Neither Triceratops had won but the circle formation had been broken and Albert's teammates milled inside the circle all looking for the coconut. In the fight the coconut had been lost or someone was hiding it.

Sensing foul play, Judge Owl lifted off his perch and flew low over the players to hoot his warning. Heavy penalties would be charged against any player or players hiding the coconut.

Hiding the coconut was a serious penalty. Any player hiding the coconut could be banished from the game..

It was a hard fought game, dinosaur tempers flared quickly, each shouting insults at the other. "Cheaters, cheaters," shouted some of Albert's team. "Crybabies," replied their opponents. "All brawn and no brains," shouted another dinosaur as insults filled the air.

During the shouting match, one of Albert's least active players, Lady May, slipped quietly to Albert's side to report she knew who had the coconut.

"Who's got it?" shouted a very loud Albert. He knew dinosaurs played rough but he couldn't believe any player on either team would pull such a rotten trick.

"The coconut, husk and all, is in the mouth of one of those meateaters. Lady May pointed her head and one foot toward three Allosaurus brothers, all with their backs turned to the players. The faces of the three Allosauruses were hidden from Albert's view although Baron Von Zack stood within a tail swish of them.

Before more could be said, the Baron, with one wild swish of his muscular tail, clobbered all three meat eaters across their backsides. The three meateaters coughed as air popped from their lungs. The coconut rolled unharmed onto the playing field, somewhat wet and slippery but still playable.

Some dinosaurs snickered. They thought it was a good joke. Others were upset, including the team captains, Prince Albert and Dangerous Dan, whose face was now caked with blood and dust. Lady May could not identify the culprit with certainty. When questioned, she said one of the meateaters had kept his mouth closed and two had kept their mouths open most of the time. Her problem was that all Allosauruses looked alike.

None of the three brothers would admit to hiding the coconut. The coconut remained in good condition and all the players were shouting, "On with the game." The team captains agreed to continue without penalties. They did ask Judge Owl to keep a close eye on the three brothers during the remainder of the game . . .

Eventually, the "coconut-inside-the-circle" plan was broken up by

The Pteranodon's toes were too short to wrap around the coconut.

Albert's tail-swishing teammates.

The King of Reptiles, Tyrannosaurus rex, though older than most, was still crafty with the coconut. Albert's team did not wish to stir his wrath. When he had control of the coconut and they wanted him to stumble, they would push one of his own teammates into his path. Thus, the mighty Tyrannosaurus rex spent half his time lecturing to his teammates to stay out of his way.

"Clear the track, clear the track," bellowed Tyrannosaurus rex to his slow-footed teammates.

Prince Albert's team spent most of the game on defense, protecting their goal with their powerful tails.

Despite the power of Tyrannosaurus rex and the meat eaters, Zack and Albert decided on a scheme to capture the coconut. Zack would attack the feet of the Triceratops who was pushing the coconut with his horns. If successful, Zack's tail would cause his horned opponent to stumble and fall. At this moment Albert would sweep in, curl his big tail around the coconut, and head for the goal line. This was Plan Z.

After playing all morning and most of the afternoon with no time out for lunch or snacks, all the dinosaurs were tired and thirsty. All had been knocked down at least once. Some had been rolled over in the dust. Their thoughts were mixed up. In fact, most of them were dazed. Tyrannosaurus himself was tired. His mouth was wide open and gasping for air. Not one of his team had cleared the track as he had so frequently requested.

"Execute Plan Z," Albert howled. He saw Zack was in po-

King Karig and Queen Violet had gathered
magnolia blossoms, leaves,
berries and fruits.

sition to bang the front feet of the Triceratops now pushing the coconut. Zack swished his tail quickly and, down went the Triceratops. Albert then curled the tip of his tail around the coconut and started galloping toward the goal. The guests cheered as they watched Albert move swiftly down the field. They saw him pass the slow Allosauruses, the Triceratops, and Tyrannosaurus rex. At last only one object stood between Albert and the goal. It was the dreaded flying Pteranodon whose feet were picking up and dropping the coconut inside the curl of Albert's tail. The Pteranodon's toes were too short to wrap around the coconut and it didn't have the knack of gripping the coconut between its legs.

Albert had thought the big bird would be given this job by Dangerous Dan. So, Albert, with one mighty flip of his tail, sent the coconut flying to the four smaller members of his clan standing near the goal. Before the flying Pteranodon knew what had happened, Andrew, May and Lynne pushed the coconut to Elizabeth standing at the edge of the goal. Elizabeth gave the coconut a quick kick and Prince Albert's team defeated the powerful and strong team led by Dangerous Dan. Albert's deep secret plan had worked. The Gunn clan, although tired, had been able to make the Big Play.

Knowing that the players would soon return to the cave tired and hungry, King Karig and Queen Violet had gathered magnolia blossoms, leaves, berries and fruits for the entire Gunn clan of Brontosauruses. These refreshments would be served whether the clan lost or won. The clan included Albert, Zack, Elizabeth, Andrew, May and Lynne. The King and Queen would have extended invitations to all the players, but some would be attending other parties. And, of course, they did not serve meat at their tables, so the meat eaters would be out of luck.

Once the food was prepared, the King and Queen went to the mouth of their cave to await the players. In the distance they heard Prince Albert and the clan approaching. The happy players were singing, "koooo koooo nut, koooo koooo nut. We won the coconut. We won the coconut."

Chapter 5

The Dinosaurs Celebrate Victory

Even though they lived millions of years ago, dinosaurs knew how to celebrate. They sang simple dinosaur songs and danced in circles.

The entire kingdom was invited to the celebration. Before the crowd arrived, the Royals had their own private party. They jumped for joy as Albert stood on his hind legs and danced what they called the Dinny Hop. They sampled all the food. They drank wild apple juice, wild grape juice, ate ginkgo leaves, magnolia blossoms and berries.

Each dinosaur told his version of the game. Each dinosaur also gave a personal account of avoiding Tyrannosaurus rex. The King and Queen were enchanted.

"Our main job," said Prince Albert, "was to keep Tyrannosaurus rex upset by his teammates, and not upset with us. We had to keep him off balance."

"Yeah, and we did not bang him with our tails," said Baron Von Zack. "But I could have."

"Tyrannosaurus rex kept howling to clear the track," chuckled Princess Elizabeth.

After a preliminary round of celebrating and eating, the young dinosaurs told King Karig and Queen Violet they would like to take a break until guests arrived. They wanted a few minutes to take the load off their feet. They wanted to appear fresh when the crowd arrived.

"We have ample room for lounging in the cave," said the King. "Yes, and we have soft nesting leaves for lying down," added Queen Violet, "if your feet and toes ache."

Nesting leaves were especially selected from birch and willow trees for their softness. Oak and maple leaves were used for lounging but pine needles were rarely used.

"My toes hurt," said Princess Elizabeth. "Ever since I kicked the coconut, my toes have felt numb."

Prince Albert said he hoped Elizabeth's toes would not stop her from doing what he had planned for the next day.

"What have you planned?" Elizabeth asked brightly, her eyes tilting open. Her curiosity showed in the way her voice lifted at the end of her question.

"I planned to invite the Merry Landers to the Red Clay Mountain," said Albert his voice deepening and his eyes glowing with excitement.

"My toes don't hurt all that much," said the alert Princess. "In fact, my toes seem to have quit hurting."

"Tell us about this Red Clay Mountain," said Baron Von Zack looking toward the floor in thought. "Lady Lynne, Lady May nor I have ever seen such a mountain."

"It's where we dinosaurs go to slide," said Prince Albert. "All the dinosaurs in the Carolina Blue Swamp country know about the slide."

"But dry clay is rough. It could hurt our tender skin," protested a cautious Lady May.

"Not this slide," Albert said with certainty. "You see, there is a deep swamp at the bottom of the mountain. Before we slide, we splash it with water from the swamp until it becomes slick as grease! It's just like sliding on oil!"

Albert assured the Merry Landers that the clay would be plenty slick and not to worry.

"When you reach the bottom of the slide, you will zoom across the lake. You'll feel like

Albert stood on his hind legs and
performed the Dinny Hop.

some giant fish skimming on the water."

"We like to zoom across water," said Zack. "We do that when we ride the ocean waves off the shores of Merry Land."

"Probably the same feeling," said Albert, "but zipping down the slippery slopes takes your breath away."

Lady Lynne and Lady May made excited sounds, catching their breath with the thought of such fun slides.

"If thinking about it makes you catch your breath," said Albert, "just wait till you try the real slides."

Chapter 6

The Pteranodons Visit Brontosaurus Cave

Prince Albert's Brontosaurus family had one of the few caves in the Carolina Blue Swamp country with ceilings high enough for the tallest dinosaur.

The Brontosauruses were tall—over 20 feet. They needed a cave as protection from the sneaky meat eaters. Without their big cave, the Brontosauruses royal family would not have survived.

The cave had a small opening. Inside it was like a large church with huge stalactites hanging from the ceiling like grand sticks of caramel candy. Inside, tunnels branched out in five directions like the points of a star.

Dinosaurs from the eastern regions liked to visit the cave of Karig to see its beauty. They also came because of its place in dinosaur history. In one of the tunnels a large flat rock became known as the Dinosaur's Rock of Fame. For thousands of years distinguished dinosaurs who visited the cave had signed their names on the dinosaur rock. It became known as the "Who's Who Reference Rock." Meat eaters had never been asked to sign the rock and, as far as Prince Albert knew, no meat eaters had been invited inside the cave; certainly none since the reign of his father, King Karig.

Prince Albert was explaining the Rock of Fame cave features to the Merry Landers when three flying Pteranodons glided to a smooth landing only a few feet away.

"Welcome to the cave of Karig," said Prince Albert. "Did you come to play *Koo Koo Nut?*"

"Yes, we flew from the Great Inland Sea," said the eldest of the Pteranodons. "Our home is 1,500 miles to the west."

"As you may have heard," said Prince Albert, "the game is over."

"But you can join us now. We are expecting more guests to help us celebrate victory," said Princess Elizabeth. "I kicked the coconut with my toe."

"It was a rough game," said Prince Albert, "and we needed some Pteranodons on our side."

The Pteranodons accepted Princess Elizabeth's invitation. They said they would have made it to the game on time but they ran into thunderstorms when crossing a range of mountains. "We had hoped to fly high and get a tail wind from the jet stream," said another Pteranodon.

"What a shame you didn't arrive sooner," said Prince Albert. "You could have joined in the fun. We did have one Pteranodon in the game on the opposite side."

"At the Great Inland Sea we're known as the 'Flying T-Birds,'" said one of the new arrivals. "Some call us the 'Dare Devil Dons!'"

"I am sometimes called a Blue Devil," said Albert.

The Pteranodons told Albert it was not such a distant flight to their home roost. They would fly east again if he called for another game. Meanwhile, they decided to come by and get acquainted. Also, if any fishing lakes or swamps were nearby, they would eat some fish to restore their energy before flying west again.

Albert replied that Brontosauruses did not eat fish and didn't go fishing, but he knew of a nearby lake where numerous fish had been seen jumping out of the water. Since his mother had a special use for fish he frequently traded fruit and berries for them.

"We're going to the fishing swamp tomorrow," said Albert. "It's a big swamp which joins the mud slides. You're welcome to join us on the slides."

"We can't slide. Our skin is too thin for mud sliding," said the eldest bird, "but we will join you. We'll fish while you slide."

Curious about all the clacking and quacking noises at the mouth of the cave, Queen Violet brought the smaller Brontosaurus clan members to the cave's mouth. They wanted to see the newcomers.

Being a polite Brontosaurus, Queen Violet lowered her large head to the ground. Then she lifted it to the eye level of the Pteranodons and said softly, "I'm Queen Violet. These are my children, nieces and nephews. The smallest is Lady Lynne." Lady Lynne dropped her head so enthusiastically she bumped her nose on a rock. In pain she extended her lower jaw and winced. An embarrassed Lady Lynne then greeted her guests.

"Our next youngest is Prince Andrew." The young prince

"We'll fish while you slide."

promptly reared himself on his strong hind legs and did a dinny hop twirling in a tight circle.

"Andrew's powerful legs will make him a premier coconut player in a few years," said Albert unable to conceal his admiration for the hopping Prince.

Andrew's jaws curved upward near his ears giving him a friendly face. He frequently stood on his hind legs and twirled to show his happiness. More reserved than her cousins, Lady May barely nodded her head as Queen Violet called her the quiet one. Baron Von Zack thumped his tail and swished it from side to side as he was introduced. The Pteranodon's could see from Zack's movement and muscular build that he would be a formidable *Koo Koo Nut* player. Princess Elizabeth had been given instruction in a kind of dance which one day would be called ballet, so she swayed daintily, shifting her weight from side to side alternately pointing the front toes of each foot towards the ground as she was introduced.

"She would rather dance than play *Koo Koo Nut*," said Albert.

The T-Birds were impressed with the life of the Brontosauruses. They couldn't remember when they had been introduced so elegantly to an entire family. Remembering that he and his father had not formally introduced themselves Prince Albert apologized. "This is my father, King Karig," said Albert who then introduced himself.

"I thought you knew our names," said Prince Albert "when you landed in front of our cave."

"We knew you were Brontosaurus leaders," quacked the eldest of the T-Birds, her long beak making the familiar clicking noise as she chopped her words. "Our parents hatched triplets and they made up our names from the Pteranodons we are. As the story goes, I was hatched first and was named Pteara. Then my brother hatched and was named Rono and my youngest brother is Don. Since we were hatched one week apart, Don is two weeks younger than I."

"That makes a lot of sense," said Prince Albert turning to his father. "I suppose my name would be something like Bronto." Then winking at his father, he said, "And Elizabeth's name would have been 'Sorry' or 'Sorrow' since we're Brontosauruses."

Few dinosaurs liked being laughed at, especially Elizabeth. "Albert, you know my name is Elizabeth," said the Princess.

"It was only a joke Elizabeth," said Albert, "only a joke."

"Please keep my name out of jokes," said Elizabeth, "But if you prefer me to call you Prince Bronto . . . " Bronto meant thunder and Brontosauruses were known as "Thunder Lizards."

"No, no, Albert's fine," said the young Prince who did not want to get into a name-calling game with his sister. "I do think the Pteranodon's have spiffy names. 'Pteara,' 'Rono' and 'Don' sound like royalty. Are you hatched from a royal line?" Albert asked.

"Oh no, no," clicked Pteara. "Our names are quite common around the Great Inland Sea. We are commoners," said Pteara, her bill clicking and clacking.

"I suppose your names are similar to 'Dino' and 'Sau' around here," said Albert.

"The Czzzar is a Brachiosaurus,
the largest of all dinosaurs."

"Although we Pteranodons are commoners," clacked Pteara, "we do have a royal line at the Great Inland Sea."

"I'll say we do," clacked Rono, "Big and royal. They think they own the sea and everything that swims in it or flies over it."

"Who rules the Great Inland Sea?" asked Prince Albert. He wanted to learn something about the western regions.

"We're under the reign of a Czzzar," said Pteara, her tongue buzzing like a bee when she pronounced the "Z" in Czar. "The Czzzar is a Brachiosaurus, the largest of all dinosaurs."

"Must be big," said Baron Von Zack his eyes widening. His tail swished back and forth with excitement. "How big is the Czar?"

"Hmmm, that's a good question," replied Pteara scratching her head with her foot. "How big is a big coconut?" asked Pteara.

"I would say it's the size of your head," said Prince Albert, "and a big coconut is heavier than two dinosaur eggs."

Pteara did some scratching in the sand outside the cave, scratched her head again and then clacked out the answer. "My estimate is the Czzzar weighs 8,500 coconuts or in mathematical terms 170 large coconut trees, or to say it another way, a small forest. The Czzzar stands tall. He can nip grapes from the tallest vines." The Pteranodons said the Czar had long front legs and a long neck. He was almost as long as a *Koo Koo Nut* field and tall as two coconut trees, with one growing on top of the other.

"What a monster," said Zack banging his tail.

"The Czzzar's wife is called the Czzzarina," clacked Pteara, "and she is as big as the Czzzar." Elizabeth tilted her head sideways and smiled as Pteara pronounced her Z's.

Chapter 7

The Mystery Egg

Queen Violet had heard quite enough from the Pteranodon named Pteara to know she was a lady of refinement and knowledge. Pteara might be just the dinosaur to answer the mystery of the abandoned egg.

"Do you know anything about dinosaur eggs?" asked Queen Violet.

"Well, we've seen a few in our travels," clacked one of the flying reptiles.

"The reason I ask is we have an abandoned egg deep in our cave," said Queen Violet, "and we would like to solve the mystery. We want to know whose egg it is and, if possible, when it was laid and how to hatch it."

"These are difficult questions," clacked Pteara, "but perhaps if we saw the egg . . . "

"Come with me," said Queen Violet, "I'll take you to the egg. She also invited the Merry Landers and her own children to follow. King Karig, also curious, followed the dinosaurs into the cave's blackness.

"The light is poor," apologized the Queen "but if you'll strap these lighted fish bladders to your head, they will help you see. The fish bladders were filled with lightning bugs. They gave off enough light for each dinosaur to follow the tail of the one ahead.

The Pteranodons had never seen fish bladder headlights.

"Ah, here it is," said Queen Violet.

They were fascinated. Pteara said such headlights might lead the way into night flying. Queen Violet had never thought about night flying, but she knew such lights helped steer through the twists and turns of the cave. She could find her own eggs after laying them at various spots in the cavern.

"How did you get lighted fish bladders," asked Rono, "since you don't eat fish?"

"We traded coconuts for them," said Queen Violet. "Some of the meat eaters also like the vegetable meat of the coconuts so they keep us supplied with fish bladders."

"Do the meat eaters stuff lightning bugs into the fish bladders?" asked Rono.

"No, this secret is only known by the Brontosaurus. This secret has been handed down from generation to generation," said Queen Violet, "but if you would like a fish bladder headlight . . . "

"We don't live in caves," said Pteara, "and we rarely fly on a moonless night, but this could change our way of life. In any case we would like one as a remembrance of our visit to this historic cave."

"You shall have it," said Queen Violet. "Each of you may keep your fish bladder strapped to your head. You can surprise the Czar when you return to the Great Inland Sea."

"I hope the bladders won't restrict our flight," said Don, who, like Lady May, had remained quiet and cautious.

"They're so small and light," said Pteara, "not nearly as heavy as carrying a fish in my beak."

"Of course not," said Don. "I suppose I was thinking about facing air currents on a long flight."

"A fish bladder filled with lightning bugs is no heavier than a toenail on your toe," said Princess Elizabeth.

All the Pteranodons felt reassured by Princess Elizabeth. They had flown with toenails on their toes from their first flight.

After a few minutes of steering their way through the cave, Queen Violet told the dinosaurs to watch each step. They were approaching the egg. "It will be lying in the middle of the cave's blackest tunnel," she said.

"Ah, here it is," said Queen Violet poking her nose close to a large white egg and sniffing it for any new smells.

Each dinosaur in turn looked at the egg, then sniffed it for possible clues on what might be inside.

Baron Von Zack, quickly said he thought the egg was an Ornithomimus. Lady May and Lady Lynne nodded their agreement. All three had seen a number of what they believed were Ornithomimus eggs in Merry Land. When hatched, many of these skinny-legged creatures had created problems. They were known as "egg suckers."

"We never guessed Ornithomimus," said Queen Violet, "since we have never seen one in the Carolina Blue Swamp country."

"Let me check it out," said Pteara as she tenderly rolled the egg with her beak.

Each of the Pteranodons took a careful look at the egg and each one listened for noises of life inside. Following a close

"If you'll strap these lighted fish bladders to your head, they will help you see.

look the three Pteranodons met a few feet away to talk over their findings.

"You know it resembles our own eggs," said Pteara clacking almost in a whisper. "I have never seen an Ornithomimus egg. Do you suppose it's one of us?"

"But the sounds inside and the vibrations are not ours," Rono replied in a whisper.

"Let me check it out," said Pteara.

"Nope, the sounds are not us," Don clacked.

"Baron Von Zack could be correct," whispered Pteara. "That's probably a small flying animal, as I do hear a pecking noise inside. It's something with a beak, and it's pecking at its own shell."

"I'm a flier and its not our egg," clacked Rono.

"Right on, Rono. It's got to be something else. And it will hatch soon, probably within two or three days." The Pteranodons nodded their heads in agreement.

"Well, what do you think?" Queen Violet asked. "Has Zack solved the mystery?"

"To the best of our knowledge, we don't know," said Pteara. "One thing is certain. The new dinosaur will hatch in a few days. We hear pecking inside."

Queen Violet turned an ear near the egg as did each of the young dinosaurs in an effort to hear the pecking. King Karig also lowered his head to listen.

"We have never seen an egg like this one," said Pteara, "but neither have we seen an Ornithomimus nest. So, we conclude it is an Ornithomimus egg."

Lady May and Lady Lynne nodded their agreement. Baron Von Zack smiled his approval. He knew an Ornithomimus egg when he saw one.

Being one of the few dinosaurs with some knowledge in the area, Prince Albert still had some doubts.

"The Ornithomimuses are fast and tricky characters," said Prince Albert. "They eat insects, fruit and small animals. But their worst habit is they eat dinosaur eggs, especially

Brontosaurus eggs. Beyond any question, they are the fastest dinosaur on the planet earth. That is why one could have run in the cave and got out without being seen. Its speed is the reason. That's the answer: speed, speed, speed!"

"How interesting," clacked Pteara who had rarely heard

King Karig lowered his head to listen.

a dinosaur speak so clearly. "Can they run as fast as we can fly?"

"That's what I'm hoping to find out. I want an Ornithomimus to play on my *Koo Koo Nut* team," Prince Albert said. "Or, if not an Ornithomimus, I want a Struthiomimus, also a swift runner."

"But if the Ornithomimus eats Brontosaurus eggs," said Queen Violet, "he'll eat all our eggs."

"Yes, and ours too, when we have them," Lady May said.

"But if the Ornithomimus eats Brontosaurus eggs," said Queen Violet, "he'll eat all our eggs."

"Ours too," said Lynne, "and that's not fair."

"If they eat all our eggs we'll become extinct," said Baron Von Zack, "and that's why I bang them with my tail in Merry Land."

"Let's look at it this way," said Prince Albert.

"The quickest way to defeat an enemy dinosaur is make him our friend," said Prince Albert.

"You're talking my language," said Lady May. "I like friends."

"But if he eats our eggs," said Queen Violet, "how can he become friendly?"

Prince Albert then explained why he thought a mystery egg was about to hatch in a Brontosaurus cave. "My opinion is this:

"The mother of this egg was in a hurry. She was hungry," Prince Albert sounded like a judge. "She came in the cave to search for food or Brontosaurus eggs, but before she could find food or an egg she laid an egg herself."

"Oh dear, oh dear," said Queen Violet, "this makes me nervous just thinking about it. I do recall seeing an Ornithomimus or Struthiomimus running away from the cave. It was only a few weeks ago. I thought nothing more about it. Those two look so much alike and both are so fast."

"Just what we need," said Prince Albert. "Just what we need on our *Koo Koo Nut* team—a player that can run fast— say 100 yards in 10 seconds. I say we should keep this speedy baby when it hatches. We'll train it to play a fast game. And, if it hatches out a Struthiomimus, it won't eat eggs."

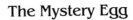

"Let's give this more thought," said King Karig.

"Yes, more thought," said Queen Violet.

"Say the word and I'll smash it with my tail," said Baron Von Zack, "and all our eggs will be safe."

"Not so fast, Zack, not so fast, this is

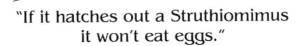

"If it hatches out a Struthiomimus it won't eat eggs."

a tough call," said Prince Albert, "This egg may be a Struthiomimus; I vote that we adopt this baby into our clan. We need a runner in the fast lane. This character could hold the coconut in his front legs and make the Triceratops, Dangerous Dan, look as slow as a tortoise."

"Should we count a dinosaur's egg before it hatches?" asked wise old King Karig.

"Up north in Merry Land we never count them. We bang them with our tails," said Zack. "We bang them before they hatch. Otherwise we would be overrun. If more and more are hatched, and if they keep eating Brontosaurus eggs, the balance of dinosaurs in Merry Land would be upset. We'd be up to our necks with those ornery Ornithomimuses."

"When you bang their eggs with your tail, they never have a chance to hatch," said Prince Albert. "Suppose you are banging a Struthiomimus egg thinking it is an Ornithomimus. This would explain why you have so many egg eaters."

"And when they grow up and eat our eggs, we don't have new baby Brontosauruses," said Lady Lynne, perking up from her drowsy mood. She had no idea Merry Landers could be cracking the wrong eggs. The problem with dinosaurs was that their brains were small, about the size of walnuts. They sometimes made mistakes without knowing their mistakes could hurt others as well as themselves.

Because Prince Albert had more brain power than most dinosaurs, he understood the problem. He said again, "One fast dinosaur is exactly what our *Koo Koo Nut* team needs."

"This one egg, be it Struthiomimus or Ornithomimus,

could make us Coast champions, if the egg hatches into a strong player."

"Let's think about it, Albert," said King Karig. "I can see you need such a fast player, but we don't need a sly creature eating our eggs before they hatch."

"I've got it," said Albert. "I've got it. We'll adopt the new one. As soon as it hatches, we'll make it one of our family. We'll teach this one to eat our food and not suck eggs. We'll feed it berries, fruits, and I'll even offer it a few magnolia blossoms." Albert's brain was doing some serious work.

The Pteranodons were fascinated with such lively and creative Brontosaurus discussions. They didn't think as deeply as the Brontosaurus. They twisted their beaks first toward Albert, then toward Zack. They couldn't be sure which side was right. None of them knew what was inside the mysterious egg.

"Let's think about this egg tomorrow," said Queen Violet. "Besides, our food is waiting. Our guests will be arriving soon. We must continue to celebrate today's victory." Food usually caused dinosaurs to forget other things.

"It's been a happy day," said Baron Von Zack. Besides, he had already eaten many of the goodies Queen Violet had placed on the flat eating rocks, and he was ready to eat again. To maintain their weight, dinosaurs spent much of their time eating.

Chapter 8

The Dinosaurs Sign Rock Of Honor

As the dinosaurs adjusted their fish bladder headlights for their return to the dining hall, Queen Violet remained as puzzled as ever about the mystery egg. Prince Albert thought Baron Von Zack and the Merry Landers were banging Struthiomimus eggs, thinking they were Ornithomimus. That is why Brontosauruses continued to lose so many eggs in Merry Land. Since neither the Pteranodons nor his own family could be certain, Albert thought it was a Struthiomimus. Yet, he could not be certain that a Struthiomimus had no egg-eating habits.

"Before we return to the food I suggest we ask our distinguished guests to place their names on the Brontosaurus Rock of Honor," said Prince Albert. A suggestion from the Prince was like a royal command. The dinosaurs were not skilled in reading or writing. Still, Prince Albert had spoken.

"Do you wish us to print or write cursively?" asked Lady Lynne. "My mother prefers the cursive style. I prefer to write with the left toe of my right front foot." Lady Lynne had her own ideas when it came to writing. For example, she never wrote with the toes of her hind feet.

Lady May actually preferred to leave a footprint since she never spent more energy than she had to. Nor did she wish to write her name on something without knowing more about it. Her father had taught her that a careless signature could be used against her.

The visiting dinosaurs had little experience in signing their names. However, not to offend Albert, they decided to scratch out some kind of signatures.

"It's easy," said Princess Elizabeth. "All you do is dip your foot or toe in the black pool of berry juice and write your name on the white Rock of Honor. Lots of dinosaurs have done it."

Baron Von Zack did not write with his toes. He used the tip of his tail. All the dinosaurs watched as Zack walked beside the Rock of Honor, dipped his tail in the black juice and printed "BVZ." "That's it," said Baron Von Zack. "That's my signature. I never write anything but my initials."

Each of the Brontosaurus Merry Landers followed Zack's lead. Lady May signed her initials, "LM." Lady Lynne, using her right foot, wrote her full name, "Lady Lynne." She especially enjoyed writing the "L." She said her mother talked of changing her name to something more beautiful, but for now she was stuck with Lynne, a name she rather liked.

The Pteranodons would have preferred to scratch an "X" on the rock, but now they realized their names were a matter of honor. If they failed to write in a cursive style, they would offend or hurt the Czar and Czarina of the Great Inland Sea. They would become the talk of the Blue Swamp dinosaurs.

"I'll go first," clacked Pteara as she dipped her right front toe in the berry juice. To everyone's surprise Pteara did not write her name. Rather she artfully scratched "T-birds" on the rock and placed her entire footprint directly beneath the writing. There was space for her two brothers to place their footprints beside hers without revealing to the Brontosaurus clan that they could not write.

"I'll go first," clacked Pteara as she dipped her right front toe in the black ink.

When all three footprints were placed side by side Prince Albert made a short speech. "Your signatures will live millions of years," Albert stated. "When dinosaurs of the future walk inside this cave they will remember that the greatest *Koo Koo Nut* players of all time lived in this cave. Their names will live on the Rock of Fame. Now the Rock has footprints from the Great Inland Sea."

Albert was quite a speaker when he got warmed up. His voice was deep and his eyes glistened with excitement.

"This is a moment of moments," Albert said, "your names will be seen for millions of years. Did you hear me? Millions of years!"

The visiting dinosaurs felt uneasy. Some of them shifted from foot to foot. With their heads shyly lowered they looked at one another. They didn't know what all the fuss was about. But, if Prince Albert said it was a moment of moments, well, so be it. They had written on rock. It was done.

What the dinosaurs wanted after this was to munch some leaves, fruit and berries. Prince Albert said "follow me. We will return to the banquet hall and food." The Prince rolled his tongue over his upper lip showing that he, too, was a normal dinosaur who liked to eat.

Because dinosaurs grew large with heavy bones, long muscles and fat they spent much of their time eating. One large dinosaur required more food than six elephants millions of years later.

Albert was a good host. He wanted the visiting dinosaurs to enjoy their stay in the Cave of Karig. Full stomachs were the key to dinosaur happiness.

Beyond full stomachs, Prince Albert thought about playful events for the following day. He wanted to be known as the "host with the most." And that is how Baron Von Zack would describe Prince Albert in the days ahead.

Prince Albert was truly "the host with the most." His name would live in dinosaur legends.

Chapter 9

The Dinosaurs Take A Break

Dinosaurs were reptiles, cold-blooded creatures. To move about with any speed they needed plenty of sunshine and heat. Many *Koo Koo Nut* games had to be called off because of clouds. Fortunately for all the reptiles, meat eaters and plant eaters alike, the game just completed had been played on a hot and sunny day.

It was a dinosaur custom following a hard-fought game for both winners and losers to celebrate by feasting. Winners ate to enhance their glory. Losers ate to renew their confidence. All reptiles looked to the sun for a time and place of feasting. On dark and cold days the reptiles' bodies became stiff and cold. When it was very cold the dinosaurs moved very slowly. Many stopped moving until the warmth of the sun made them feel normal. So most reptiles spent a lot of time either warming up or cooling off.

Because Prince Albert's royal family lived in a large heated cave, they could move around even on cool days. Heat came up into the cave from the boiling hot springs beneath the flat rocks of the floor.

Following any *Koo Koo Nut* game Prince Albert's team-mates called for a celebration. The guests at the game knew the royal cave was warm and food was plentiful. Winning di-nosaurs could eat well into the night.

Chapter 10

The Meat Eaters Seek Revenge

The losing team, captained by Dangerous Dan, the Triceratops, also called for a feast. They were not as enthusiastic as the winners. Three meat eating Allosauruses on the losing team were very unhappy. They were named in the order they were hatched, Allo, Sau and Rus. Sau's name had been changed to Sorry and Russ to Rusty. Allo was often called Big Al because he was the largest of the vicious reptiles.

Big Al was in the mood for a feast all right. His food choice was the royal clan of Brontosauruses, especially the three younger ones who were not able to defend themselves. Also Big Al wanted to make up for losing the game. What better way for a meat-eating reptile than take a few bites from the winners.

When Big Al reached a corner of the playing field beyond the hearing of the Tyrant King, Tyrannosaurus rex, he called his brothers to him. He wanted to get them in a fighting mood, a job which usually required very little effort.

Big Al began by saying he felt lousy.

"So do I," said a dejected Sorry. His voice sounded pitiful.

"Me too," said Rusty, "I don't feel so good."

Then Big Al began talking against Prince Albert. He asked if Sorry and Rusty had not seen Tyrannosaurus rex go to the middle of the playing field and congratulate that royal bum, Prince Albert? All three agreed they wanted to get even. They wanted to wipe those smiles off the faces of the winners.

"But what about the promise Tyrannosaurus rex made to Prince Albert," said Rusty. "He said we would not bite during the game."

"The game is over," said Big Al. "All bets are off. We are not bound by any rules or promises of Tyrannosaurus rex. From now on it's back to the laws of the jungle."

"What do you suggest?" asked Al's middle brother, Sorry.

"I say we take a bite out of those young Brontosauruses who played against us," said Big Al.

"Good thinking, Allo," said Sorry, calling his brother by his official name.

"Maybe two or three biters," said Rusty.

"Good thinking," said Big Al.

Then to the meat eaters' surprise, one of Prince Albert's bodyguards, a Stegosaurus named Captain Stego, walked into the middle of the meat eater's secret meeting.

"Not so fast, not so fast," hissed Captain Stego in a threatening whisper. "I'm Prince Albert's protector. I heard it all."

"So what," said Big Al. But he did look at the four sharp horns protruding from the Stegosaurus' tail.

"It's a dumb idea," Stego hissed. His small, dark, dry and unblinking eyes stared directly into the eyes of Big Al.

Big Al did not like this insult. He then scolded Stego on his rudeness for listening to their meeting. Was there no honor left among the so-called royal bodyguards? Big Al said such conduct would lead the dinosaur world to ruin.

"We commoners expect more from the royals and their trusted servants such as you," said Big Al.

"Rubbish, utter garbage," hissed Stego. "Your kind disgraces dinosaurs."

Big Al's blood was running hot. His words went out of control. "One more job like this and we'll nip off your head, all in one bite."

Not easily bluffed, Stego kept his cool, his small dark eyes still unblinking. Captain Stego had been well selected as royal bodyguard.

"Over the horns of my dead tail," hissed Stego. Then he made a few more scary remarks. He said the mouth of the royal cave was littered with the bones of meat eaters who thought they could bite off the head of a Stegosaurus.

"Don't let my small head deceive you," warned Stego. "I have more sharpness in my tail than you have in your head." Stego calmly nodded to the four sharp horns protruding from his tail. Each horn was three feet long.

The Stegosaurus soon realized the meat eaters were not listening to his tough talk. "Besides," he said, "if the meat eaters were serious about taking a bite of royal flesh, they could try their luck tomorrow."

"Why tomorrow?" asked Big Al.

Knowing Prince Albert's plan to visit the mud slides the following day, Captain Stego gave Big Al a foolish offer.

"When the sun reaches mid-morning's warmth," said

Stego, "the royal dinosaurs will travel to the mud slides. They will be protected by their royal bodyguards, including myself. If you and your brothers think you are bold and clever enough, you can give us a try. I can tell you now we'll give you a horning you'll remember."

The Allosaurus brothers did not take such a challenge lightly. The Stegosaurus was foolish enough to reveal the trail Prince Albert would use. Big Al knew what to do about it. Captain Stego should not have told the meat eaters where a Brontosaurus planned to travel the following day.

Big Al smiled at his brothers. "Meat eater is my name and fighting is my game." Rusty and Sorry nodded approvingly.

Prince Albert had no idea his number one bodyguard, Captain Stego, would say such risky things to those trashy meat eaters, especially Big Al and his brothers.

When the threats stopped Captain Stego walked off to join the royal family on their way to the royal cave for a celebration.

Because Stego felt sure of himself as a fighter, he never mentioned his conversation with Big Al to Prince Albert, or to anyone, especially the part about going to the mud slides the following day. But a Stegosaurus only had a brain the size of a walnut.

Chapter 11

Dinosaurs Feast

During the talk between Stego and Big Al, Prince Albert had gone about the playing field seeing his friends. He invited plant eaters, as well as all the visiting guests, to join him at the Cave of Karig for a royal feast. The Prince's mother, Queen Violet had prepared a good feast. Prince Albert said that the royal cave would be filled with ginkgo leaves, grapes, magnolia blossoms, tender leafy ferns, fruits and berries of the season.

Meat eaters could not come to the celebration because the feast was all vegetables and fruits. Besides, the meat eaters could not be trusted when rubbing shoulders with royal Brontosauruses. Such togetherness would tempt the meat eaters.

The celebration in the royal cave developed into the kind of lively party dinosaurs relished.

Prince Albert began the fun by performing one of his own dances, the Dinny Hop. This dance would remain famous for many years. Princess Elizabeth, and Ladies Lynne and May, wearing bright red toenail polish, danced the Royal Dinosaur Ballet. They danced to the rhythm of Baron Von Zack's tail making sounds as his tail pounded a large stalactite. The ballet pleased most of the guests, who asked where they might find some red toenail polish. Lady Lynne did a solo dance skipping sideways in a circle. She sang, "Look, Pa, I'm Dancing." She always took care to keep to the rhythm of the Baron's tail.

During her first two years, Lady Lynne had received special dancing and singing instructions from her mother. Lady May could also sing and dance but she was too shy to do it by herself. Lady May saw that many of the dinosaurs had musical throats. When not busy with their berries, grapes and leaves they sang a musical version of "koooo koooo nut." At one point Prince Andrew joined the singing, only to get a quick shush from Prince Albert.

"Quiet, Andrew," said Prince Albert, "or you'll call another game of *Koo Koo Nut* before we're rested."

None of the dinosaurs were interested in another game before they rested and recovered from the game they just played.

Judge Owl, Chief of the Jungle's Judiciary, closed out the celebration by dancing to the song, "Who Who Done It." "Who who done it," sang the Judge. "The Brontos done done done it. They won, won won, it." Judge Owl did stutter, but

"Who Who Done It," sang the Judge.

the guests could not decide if he was stuttering or if it was words to the music. In any case, the guests clapped a lot when Judge Owl finished. It was quite different from anything he had ever done. In court he was always very proper.

Prince Albert ended the celebration by inviting all the guests to join him and his cousins at the mud slides the next day. The Pteranodons from the Great Inland Sea had already accepted a special invitation since as they had arrived too late to play *Koo Koo Nut.*

Overnight guests of the royal household, including the three Brontosaurus cousins from Merry Land and the three Pteranodons from the Great Inland Sea, joined the Royal family on their sleeping slabs in a dark hallway deep in the cave. Dinosaur-sleeping slabs were large flat rocks under which could be heard the gurgling of warm mineral springs. Steam from the springs was good for the dinosaurs' noses and it relaxed them after a *Koo Koo Nut* game.

Whether it was the gurgling sounds or the steam from the springs, all the dinosaurs awoke well-rested with bright eyes. They looked forward to the mud slides.

Chapter 12

Come Alive!
Come Alive!

Prince Elizabeth was the first dinosaur to wake up. She lost no time in singing out, "Come alive, come alive, we are the dinosaur five," as she did every morning to the Royal family. Then she sang out, "This is the day we dinosaurs go to picnic." The dinosaurs were still stretching.

When they reached the cave's opening, Prince Albert gave final instructions for the day. The prince said it was about five miles from the cave to the mud slides. If all went well, and there were no foot blisters or accidents, the dinosaurs should arrive in two hours. This meant their column would walk no faster than two and one half miles per hour, about half the speed used in *Koo Koo Nut.*

"We don't want you to be footsore from walking before we reach the slides," Prince Albert said jokingly, "and rub all the gold dust off your feet. We don't want meat eaters on our trail."

Prince Albert went on to say the dinosaurs would be guarded by four of the royal family's best Stegosauruses, led by their captain, Captain Stego. If any of the dinosaurs saw any danger they should sing out. They didn't have to worry about any grazing plant eaters along the jungle trail. But if they spotted a meat eater, they were to shout "Meat eater to the left," "Meat eater to the right" or "Meat eater dead ahead."

Captain Stego wanted to tell about his talk of the previous day with the meat eaters, but decided it might upset Prince Albert. Captain Stego was loyal to the Royal family but not to the point of getting himself in trouble with the Prince.

"When we reach the slides there will be no tail first sliding," said the Prince. "Head first only. Bottom sliding is okay, but no tail firsts. Any questions?" asked Prince Albert.

Since the Pteranodons were flying reptiles, they were not eager for a five-mile hike. Their feet simply were not built for walking such long distances.

"Would it be asking too much, your highness," said the commoner Pteara, "if my brothers Rono and Don and I flew slightly ahead of your column. We could circle above if you like and help Captain Stego spot meat eaters."

"That would be fine," said Albert. "How thoughtless of me to forget that you are fliers, not walkers."

"Sure enough," Prince Albert continued, "now that I think about it, you Pteranodons may not find the mud slides as exciting as a steep dive."

Pteara smiled and clacked to her brothers that Prince Albert was both smart and polite. Perhaps they should make him a member of the T-birds.

"Any more questions or comments?" asked Albert. There were none. Prince Albert moved to the front of the column and asked Captain Stego to take a position ahead of him. He posted one guard to the right and one to the left of the column's middle. The fourth guard was on the rear of the column to prevent any attacks from behind. Captain Stego had a different

Prince Albert asked the dinosaurs to
fall in line according to their strength.

plan in mind for the bodyguards: two on either side of the column, two in front and two in the rear.

Prince Albert then asked the dinosaurs to fall in line according to their strength. "Baron Von Zack will follow me, then Prince Andrew and Princess Elizabeth. Lady May and Lady Lynne will bring up the tail of the column," he explained.

Prince Albert thought this march would be a good time to train dinosaurs. He wanted to teach them how to defend themselves if they met meat eaters. Baron Von Zack didn't think he needed this special instruction. After all, he had safely led Lady May and Lady Lynne over the long route from Merry Land. Still Zack was willing to learn a few things from the prince he admired.

Baron Von Zack had one solution to any attackers—bang them quickly with his tail. So far he had sent a number of meat eaters reeling in full retreat. Their legs were very weak when they felt the powerful swish of a Brontosaurus' tail.

Chapter 13

Ambush on the Trail

While Prince Albert and the Brontosauruses slept, Al and his bandit brothers took up their attack position along the one jungle trail connecting the royal cave to the mud slides. The best spot for an attack was a ravine through which the Brontosauruses had to walk. It was a long, narrow ditch about as wide as a Brontosaurus' belly.

With any luck, each Allosaurus hiding on the bank of the ravine would be able to step or jump to the back of one of Prince Albert's clan.

Big Al and his brothers hid themselves in tall grasses and giant leafy ferns. None of the bodyguards suspected an attack. They heard and saw nothing but a few plant eaters grazing in the distance. Nor did the Pteranodons flying above see any signs of danger.

As Prince Albert's carefree brother and sister entered the ravine, they swayed to the tune of Princess Elizabeth's wake-up call. "Come alive, come alive, we are the Dinosaur five." Prince Albert changed his words. He alone was singing, "we are the dinosaur six." Six was the number in his column. Six didn't rhyme with alive but who cared?

The ravine turned out to be a lot wider than Big Al and his brothers expected. Either the ditch was wider or the Brontosauruses' bodies were smaller than the killers thought.

"Don't let the smallness of my head
deceive you," warned Captain Stego.

The Brontosauruses marched cheerfully into the trap thinking it was no more than a vine-covered path. The Royal guardsmen under Captain Stego were caught up in the marching song. They had forgotten their duty of spotting meat eaters hidden along the trail.

The all-out attack came like the sound of rolling thunder from the mouths of Big Al, Sorry and Rusty. With their jaws opened wide, each showing a mouthful of teeth, they let out a roar and jumped toward the first three dinosaurs in column, Prince Albert, Baron Von Zack and Prince Andrew. Captain Stego and his three bodyguards charged to the rescue, but they couldn't reach the meat eaters, whose feet had landed on the Brontosauruses backs. The meat eaters had then fallen head first toward the ground and were wedged upside down between the side of the ditch and the sides of Albert, Zack and Andrew.

Prince Albert didn't move. Baron Von Zack was trying to reach the meat eating monsters with his tail. Zack's trouble was he couldn't move his tail into a banging position. Neither could Prince Andrew. Each Allosaurus was upside down and wedged between a Brontosaurus and the wall of the ditch.

Thanks to Captain Stego's long training, he saw a possible solution. "Push the meat eaters against the wall. Press, push, press sideways, said Stego in a hissing tone. This was easily heard by all the dinosaurs.

Thus far, except for a few claw marks near their spines, the backs of the Brontosauruses were not seriously injured.

"Push sideways, push sideways," again hissed Captain Stego. The Brontosauruses caught on quickly. Before the

"Push the meat eaters against the wall.
Press, push, press sideways," said Stego.

meat eaters could wiggle their legs to the ground, they had the breath pushed from their lungs. When Captain Stego saw the bandits' legs go limp, he knew the Brontosauruses had won. Quietly he told Prince Albert to begin his march again.

From the sky the Pteranodons never realized an ambush had taken place in the ravine. They noted scratches on the backs of three and asked if they had encountered thorn trees.

"Thorn trees, indeed," said Prince Albert, who gave the Pteranodons a full report on the attack.

Chapter 14

On to the Slides

"Will we continue to the mud slides?" Pteara inquired.

"Certainly," said Prince Albert. "We never allow meat eaters to spoil our plan for the day. We always stay cool."

"You speak like a true member of the Gunn clan," said Baron Von Zack. "If they approach us again, we'll give them another dose of our royal medicine."

"You mean we'll bang them with our tails," said Princess Elizabeth.

"You've got it," said the Baron whose tail involuntarily swished to and fro when he thought about it. The dinosaur column paused on top of the ridge just above the mud slides. All the dinosaurs eyes stared at the actions below.

Never had Prince Albert seen so many different kinds of dinosaurs gathered at the mud slides.

Prince Albert noted a number of unidentified dinosaurs at the slides, including at least three Allosauruses, that he did not know. He asked his own clan if they wanted to return to the cave or continue to the slides. After all, it was up to Prince Albert to keep them safe; and he couldn't count on Captain Stego.

"Let's go for the slides," said Baron Von Zack. He was full of confidence after defeating the recent ambush and after winning the *Koo Koo Nut* game the day before. "If they attack again, we'll bang them with our tails."

Albert had no worries for himself, nor for Baron Von Zack. He knew the two of them could overpower the best of what they saw. Yet he was worried that Lady May or Lady Lynne, or Prince Andrew or even Princess Elizabeth would get into trouble.

Prince Albert scratched his head on a tree as he thought about the dangers.

"It's dicey," said Prince Albert.

"What do you mean by dicey?" asked Elizabeth.

"I mean it's a bit dangerous."

"You mean, if we slide we'll be taking a chance?"

"Let me tell you how it is," said Prince Albert. "I have counted more than 20 dinosaurs using the slides. Most are friendly plant eaters. I have seen two Brachiosauruses, the largest of all dinosaurs. They are plant eaters like us, and they eat about 2,000 pounds of food each day. They devour magnolia leaves like daisies. But then, I'm sure I spotted two and maybe three Allosaurus meat eaters—the same as those that ambushed us in the ravine."

"Whoeee, Whoeee," snorted Lady May and Lady Lynne. "What excitement! Will they bite us?"

"How about those we pushed in the ditch?" drooled Prince Andrew.

"Perhaps, yes" said Prince Albert. "Perhaps, no. I can see three Allosauruses down by the water walking on their hind legs. As you can see they move slowly. They walk slowly but they have wide, powerful jaws and a mouthful of sharp teeth. We also know they have sharp claws. I assure you they can swallow big chunks of meat, too."

"Whoeee, whoeee, whoeee," gasped the young Brontosauruses, squirming and looking at the fat on their hind legs and tails.

"In the *Koo Koo Nut* game we gave them a good banging," said Baron Von Zack. "And we gave them a good squeeze in the ditch. If they try anything, we'll bang them again."

Prince Albert squinted his eyes for a better view of all the dinosaurs. He could see two Brachiosauruses plainly. They were taller and longer than the others. They were standing in the water. They, like the Brontosauruses,

"Right on, mates," said Albert, kicking one leg in the air.

spent much of their time in lakes and rivers.

"Remember this," said Albert, "meat eaters rarely attack while we're in the water. They live off the land. They don't like water."

Zack said the Merry Landers had never been with so many different kinds of dinosaurs. Then his nostrils flared. "If those meat eaters aren't careful, we'll take them for a swim they won't forget."

"Could we distract them with our clacking beaks?" asked Rono.

"We could peck them too," said Don warming to the defense of the plant eaters.

"Right on, mates," said Albert, kicking one leg in the air and lifting his tail. "We are better swimmers and fliers. In the water, we plant eaters can sink meat eaters. Fliers can make problems for meat eaters."

Chapter 15

Final Instructions

Before Albert signalled his group to proceed to the slides he gave some final instructions. "If a meat eater comes close hit the slide and head for deep water. Never go down the slides tail first. I repeat to all dinosaurs, no sliding tail first." None of the dinosaurs questioned Prince Albert's direction, but the young ones thought tail first might be fun.

Because so many dinosaurs were at the lake, the Brontosaurus clan was not worried. As they approached the slide, they were full of fun and forgot their fears. Never had they seen such a grand parade of dinosaurs. They knew this would be a day to remember. So what if some old Allosauruses were stalking around? Plant eaters in such numbers could overcome any threat. Meat eaters at the lake just made the adventure more thrilling.

Still, the Pteranodons were none too happy about the Allosauruses. If the meat eaters didn't swim and didn't care for water, what were they doing at the slides?

"The Allosauruses are here to nip at the plant eaters,"Pteara clacked. "And they might want to bite me and my brothers."

"Guard your wings and tail," Albert warned the Pteranodons. "I don't think they will attack your beak or your head."

Before Albert could finish his final instructions about keeping their noses high as they entered the water Zack went

Before Albert could finish his instructions
Zack went zipping down the slide.

zipping down the slide . He looked liked a blue-green streak. After counting ten, Elizabeth went next, then May, then Andrew, then Lynne. Albert stood at the top of the slide telling other dinosaurs to stand clear until his clan had made its first slide. Then Albert made a run and hit the slick red clay as he had done so often. Each hit the water with a giant splash sending sprays of water in a big circle. What fun! What wonderful fun!

What fun! What wonderful fun!

Chapter 16

The Plant Eaters Meet

After a few slides, Prince Albert took a break to chat with a nearby Brachiosaurus standing in the midst of falling water brought about by dinosaurs splashing into the lake. Water splashes cooled the neck and body of the giant Brachiosaurus. His skin felt the heat of a scorching sun.

"Hi, Matey," said Albert. Matey was a term used by friendly plant eaters during greetings and sometimes during conversation.

"How long you been sliding?" Albert continued.

"Since the mid-morning sun," said the Brachiosaurus. Dinosaurs used the sun to determine the time of day. "Got here a few minutes before your group looked down on us from the top of the ridge."

"For a few moments we thought you might be the royals arriving," said the Brachiosaurus. "But we didn't see any crowns or royal sashes, so we assumed you were commoners."

"So that's why you're here?" asked Prince Albert. "You came to see the royals?"

"You got it, Matey," said the Brachiosaurus.. "Both my brother and I came to have a look. That's why you see so many dinosaurs hanging about." The Brachiosaurus explained that some of the dinosaurs attending yesterday's royal cave celebration had spread the word far and wide that the royals were coming to the slides today.

"So why did you come, Matey?" asked the Brachiosaurus of Albert. "Did you want a glimpse of the royals as well?" "Matey, I am a royal," said Prince Albert. "I'm the Crown Prince."

Doubtful of what Albert had said, the Brachiosaurus said jokingly, "Yeah and I'm Brocky, King of Kings."

Albert smiled at the joke. His smile turned into a frown. He had a problem. Should he, or should he not tell the Brachiosaurus who he really was? Prince Albert had brought his clan to the slides for a day of fun. He hadn't planned any royal duties.

Looking down on Albert's back, the Brachiosaurus said, "If you're a Prince then how did you get all those scratches on your back? I've seen scratches on your buddies as well."

"Allosaurus scratches," said Albert. "I got them on the trail this morning." Albert suddenly decided to say no more. If the Brachiosaurus didn't know a Prince when he saw one, so be it. Still, it seemed a pity that there were so many commoners at the slides who would never know they had been in the company of royals.

As Albert left the side of the Brachiosaurus, the Prince said he too would keep an eye out for the royals. The Brachiosaurus warned Albert to keep an eye on the meat eaters. He had counted three and there could be more.

The tall Brachiosaurus also kept an eye on Albert as the Prince left for the slides. It was just possible that he was the

Prince. Meanwhile, at the top of the slides, Prince Albert called the royal clan into a huddle to explain why so many dinosaurs were milling about. "They've come to see us," whispered the Prince.

Meanwhile, the Brachiosaurus, who jokingly claimed he was king

"If you're a Prince, then how did you get all those scratches on your back?"

of kings, called his brother to his side.

"That Brontosaurus claims he's a Prince," said the giant of reptiles. "But how can one tell for sure? I told him I was Brocky, king of kings." Both Brachiosauruses chuckled and then gave the six Brontosaurus royals a close look. They did not really know how to tell a royal.

"Do you think crowns grow from their heads?" asked one of the brothers, "or should they be wearing halos?"

"Beats me, I'm mixed up," replied the other giant reptile.

Other dinosaurs eyed the two giants whose heads reached as high as the top of the mud slides. Both Brachiosauruses showed a lot of interest in the movements of the six Brontosauruses. As a result everyone at the lake started saying that royals were present.

With all the talk, Princess Elizabeth said they should tell who they were. Baron Von Zack agreed. So did Lady Lynne. Lady May didn't know. She was worried that the royals might be attacked by enemies or stampeded by friends if the others found out.

Five of the six Royals said they should say they were royals or else the commoners might think royalty was ashamed of itself.

Prince Albert then made another call on the two giant Brachiosauruses who were still standing together. Wading directly in front of the two giants Prince Albert lowered his head as he had been taught by King Karig. The King had taught all members of the royal family to be humble in front of commoners.

"Begging your pardon once more," Prince Albert said to the giants. "The members of my royal clan have decided to say who we are. I am Prince Albert. With me are my younger brother Andrew and my sister Princess Elizabeth. We are children of King Karig and Queen Violet. Joining us at the slides today are three royal cousins from Merry Land, Baron Von Zack, Lady May and Lady Lynne. Circling overhead are three Pteranodons from the Great Inland Sea. They are commoners, subjects of the Czar and Czarina. They arrived too late to play *Koo Koo Nut* and have stayed for a few days as guests of the royal family."

Both Brachiosaurus brothers were impressed. They lowered their heads to the Prince.

"We are honored, your highness," said one. "Can we help?"

"Could you quietly tell the others," said Prince Albert "to form large circles at the foot of the slides where we'll talk to them and thank them for coming."

Chapter 17

Circles of Commoners

The Brachiosauruses lost no time in spreading the word to the other dinosaurs. The commoners were told to form large circles near the slides to meet the royals.

No meat eaters were invited since plant eaters were not friendly with cannibals. If a few meat eaters tried to join the circles, they would be watched by Prince Albert's four Stegosaurus bodyguards. The royal family also counted on the two giant Brachiosauruses for protection although they were not good fighters.

Despite their curiosity about royals, most visiting dinosaurs were none too friendly with each other. From their day of hatching, they had lived competitive lives in search of food. As they became adults, most dinosaurs had forgotten their manners. They routinely snapped or pushed at one another without having a reason.

The first group of commoners formed a circle promptly as they had been told. It included a family of web-footed duckbilled Anatosauruses. They had been swimming near the mud slides listening to Prince Albert and the Brachiosauruses talk. The duckbills dared not stray far from the safety of the water when meat eaters were near. Meat eaters could not swim.

After losing out in the ravine attack, Big Al, Sorry and Rusty had found new energy and followed the royals to the slides. Allosauruses always made plant eaters nervous. Besides, Big Al, Sorry and Rusty and at least one other meat eater, an Albertosaurus, walked around the slides. He had chased the duckbills. He too was slowly making his way to the circle to watch the royal family.

The Albertosaurus was only a nuisance to a nearby Ankylosaurus. Looking like a giant tortoise, the Ankylosaurus couldn't draw back its feet and head when under attack. The Albertosaurus felt teased by such a slow-moving creature. He energetically clawed at the armored Ankylosaurus, trying to overturn it, but he couldn't. The Ankylosaurus kept telling the meat eater to get lost, but he kept moving into the circle beside the armored plant eater. Finally, the Ankylosaurus gave the Albertosaurus a furious whack with his tail. The tail, with its large lumps, knocked the meat eater to the ground. Prince Albert's Stegosaurus bodyguards surrounded the Albertosaurus. They told him to mind his manners or they would chase him from the circle.

When the grumbling and quarreling among dinosaurs had subsided, Prince Albert entered the large circle. He introduced himself and each member of the royals. Then he led the royal column into places where they could talk with each dinosaur. Each royal would say some word or phrase such as "Welcome," "Thanks for coming," or "Have a nice day."

The commoners replied with such phrases as, "Good show Matey," and "You'd be welcome in my grazing area anytime." One female Brontosaurus looking into Prince Albert's eyes said, "What a lovely creature, what a lovely neck." Prince Albert gave her his royal smile. He was surprised by all the different kinds of plant eaters living so near the royal cave.

First in the circle was a long-tailed Diplodocus. "I'm Dippy," he said. "Nice of you to come," said Prince Albert, admiring the length of the Diplodocus tail.

"I'm Anky, the Ankylosaurus."

"I'm Struthy," a Struthiomimus said.

When Albert passed the Albertosaurus, the meat eater said with a toothy grin, "I'm Albert. Some ask if I'm

Resembling a giant tortoise,
the Ankylosaurus was unable to draw back
its feet and head when under attack.

of royal blood since I have your name."

"Albert's a good name" said the smiling Prince. "You should give up eating meat and become a vegetarian."

"I can't survive on jungle spinach," said the Albertosaurus. "You ought to join us meat eaters."

"Thank you," said the Prince, "for your words. But dinosaurs are as different as the sun and the moon."

The Albertosaurus thought he could never again chase or bite a Brontosaurus without remembering Prince Albert's words about the sun and moon.

When Prince Albert finished talking to all the dinosaurs in the circle he turned to ask the other royals to leave with him. To Albert's surprise, only Baron Von Zack and Prince Andrew were following him.

Looking across the circle Albert saw Princess Elizabeth, Lady May and Lady Lynne talking to three handsome male Brontosauruses. The royal ladies' heads bobbed up and down as did the heads of the commoners. "I wonder what they are doing?" asked Prince Albert.

"I must put a stop to this. First thing you know those commoners will be wanting to marry into the royal family.

"The commoners need a good tail banging," said Baron Von Zack. "They should know better."

Chapter 18

The Meat Eaters Attack

Circle after circle of dinosaurs gathered to greet the royals. It was a happy moment in dinosaur history. The commoners were most interested in the royals, but they wanted to know how to tell a royal from a commoner.

"Next time, I'll wear my royal sash," Albert replied. That answer satisfied the commoners.

Following the ceremonies, Prince Albert noted Big Al and his two pirate brothers were staying too close for comfort. Since they were still angry or hungry, or both, Albert asked Captain Stego to bring up more security guards when the Allosauruses neared the slides.

Baron Von Zack saw the meat eaters closing in on a Diplodocus. He told Albert that Dippy's tail was in danger.

"They're closing on Dippy's tail," shouted Zack. "Swat them quickly," honked the Baron. "Swat them with your tail."

All the sauropods, including Diplodocus, Brontosaurus and Brachiosaurus, had small brains. Their tails and hind legs were favorite spots for meat eaters to attack.

"You're right Zack, they're going after Dippy," said Albert. "I guess it's because so many of them live around here."

Although quick and cunning, one Diplodocus could not escape the rush of three meat eaters all diving for the plant

121

eater's long tail. Dippy saw them coming but all he did was check his front legs to make sure he was standing in deep water, too deep for them to attack his neck. Meanwhile, Dippy forgot about his tail, all 50 feet of it lying on the beach.

"Hey, Dippy, swish your tail," Baron Von Zack shouted. But it was too late. The Allosauruses had pounced on a large chunk of Dippy's tender tail, biting off a piece as long as a snake.

Allosauruses were usually afraid of the whipping tail of a Diplodocus, but, in this case, the meat eaters worked quickly. They enjoyed their first snack since the *Koo Koo Nut* game the day before.

Out of concern for a fellow plant eater, Prince Albert and the two Brachiosauruses went over to check the Diplodocus' tail. Dippy said not to worry. "I can grow a new tail," he said.

As Prince Albert came back to his clan he passed another duckbill-type dinosaur called a Trachodon.

"What happened to the Dippy?" asked the Trachodon.

"He lost part of his tail," said Prince Albert, "but he thinks he can grow another."

The Trachodon turned to check his own tail. Opening his mouth he showed about 2,000 small white teeth which he used to grind twigs and seeds.

"If that Dippy had my webbed feet," said the Trachodon, "he could swim fast and still have his tail."

"He sure could," said Prince Albert, "but we can't be too careful when three hungry Allosauruses decide they want to make a meal out of our tail."

"None of us can be too careful," agreed the giant Brachiosaurus.

"They're closing on Dippy's tail,"
shouted Zack.

Chapter 19

Young Dinosaurs Disobey

The young Brontosauruses had seen the meat eaters attack. They had heard Prince Albert's warning, but they were too busy having fun to worry about the Diplodocus' tail.

After many slides the younger dinosaurs, May, Andrew and Lynne decided it was time to try a slide tail first. They knew Prince Albert had warned against it. Still, a slide tail first should be an even greater thrill. These three simply decided that even a spill might be fun on a slide.

Albert glanced up just as all three turned their tails down the slippery slope. They were coming down tail first—the worst kind of sliding.

"Turn around, turn around," Albert howled, his huge jaws wide open, his eyes staring in fright.

"Head first, head first," Elizabeth hooted, "You're supposed to slide head first. You're sliding into danger."

Baron Von Zack stood by to watch, curious to see what happened. Actually he had been thinking about sliding tail first, but he decided to obey Albert's rules.

Neither Albert nor Elizabeth could stop the three younger dinosaurs from sliding tail first. Visiting dinosaurs stopped in their tracks when they saw what was happening. Older dino-

They were coming down tail first
—the worst kind of sliding.

saurs knew that sliding tail first was a no-no. What they didn't know was how much damage could be done.

"Clear the landing area, clear the landing area," shouted one Brachiosaurus, a good swimmer.

Albert knew the young Brontosauruses were in serious trouble. He moved as close as he could to the landing area without getting too close. The Trachodon, being one of the best swimmers of all dinosaurs, swam close to Albert.

The dinosaurs' tail-first slide was really thrilling. They honked and hooted all the way down. "Whoeee, Whoeee, Whoeee," they screeched. Then it happened. Their tails hit the water in a down position forcing their bodies to flip over on their backs. They were upside down.

What a sight. Three young dinosaurs belly up. Their mouths chug-chugged water, and they coughed and sputtered as water kept pouring through their mouths into their long necks.

When a Brontosaurus went belly-up, its back acted like the keel of a ship. No matter how much the young dinosaurs squirmed, kicked and struggled to right themselves their backs remained low in the water.

Being afraid for their lives, Prince Albert shouted, "Push them ashore. All dinosaurs push." The Brontosauruses were not built for pushing. They could lean against something, such as a tree, with all their weight, and chances were the tree would fall. But it was not all that easy to lean against three floundering youngsters. Neither were the Brachiosauruses good pushers. The Trachodons with duckbills could help. They could get their long bills beneath most floating objects.

In this case, however, only one Trachodon was near. With its long duckbill under Lady Lynne, it slowly moved her ashore leaving the other two gulping water.

Baron Von Zack told the two Brachiosauruses, the two Diplodocuses (including the one with part of his tail bitten off) and Prince Albert to make waves. If all made sweeping motions with their tails, it might make large waves that would work like an incoming tide.

"Large waves," said Baron Von Zack, "should wash them to shore."

Zack had seen large waves wash whales ashore near his home in Merry Land. When whales swam too near a breaking surf, the water became more powerful than the whales.

"It's worth a try," said Prince Albert as all the large dinosaurs positioned themselves to make waves with their strong tails.

It seemed like hours, but actually it took only a few minutes. The six dinosaurs positioned themselves around the victims, their tails pointing toward Lady May and Prince Andrew. The floundering Brontosauruses were still flailing and kicking the air with their feet.

"On the count of one," said Prince Albert, "we will lift our tails. On the count of two, we will drop them in the water. With the count of three, four, and five we will push water to make the first wave. Then with the count of one we will lift our tails and repeat the process. Any questions?"

"Who will do the counting?" Zack asked.

"We all count," said Albert. "Everybody counts. Ready

with your tails. Count . . . One . . .
two . . . three, four, five. Repeat . . .
One . . . two . . . three, four, five."

The Pteranodons had been
quietly fishing on the
other side

They were upside down. Water kept
pouring through their mouths
into their long necks.

of the lake, but hearing the commotion near the slides, decided to fly over and have a look.

Chapter 20

The Pteranodons in Action

The Pteranodons had not realized the three young dinosaurs they had met the night before were in serious danger until they started flying in a circle above the action.

"How frightful," clacked Pteara, "Terrible." From the air the dinosaurs' tails resembled floating logs they had seen in the Great Inland Sea. It was no longer fun and games. The Pteranodons saw a battle below. Their lives were in danger. Adult dinosaurs were fighting to save the youngsters.

"Plant eaters are not dumb," clacked Pteara, "They're making waves. Looks like a storm on the Great Inland Sea."

"It's no wonder they win at *Koo Koo Nut*," said Rono. "They help each other. They are loyal; they're fighters. They fight to win." They would report to the Czar when they returned to the Great Inland Sea that the eastern plant eaters were strong, brave and caring.

As the waves grew larger and larger everyone knew Zack's idea was working. The Pteranodons had never seen such wave-making. Such huge waves would wash anything ashore. What the flying reptiles could not see though, was the condition of the youngsters.

Soon the waves were no longer needed. The Trachodon and one of the Stegosaurus bodyguards had proved helpful.

Their snouts had created a rocking motion causing the three young accident victims to wash ashore. Now all three were lying ashore on their sides with their long necks lower than their chests so that water could drain from their lungs. Water gushed from their mouths as dinosaurs took turns pressing their feet on the water-logged lungs.

In all this turmoil, the plant eaters did not see the three Allosauruses creeping toward the three young dinosaurs. These were the same ones, Allo, Sorry and Rusty, who had lost the *Koo Koo Nut* game and tried to attack. The meat-eating brothers knew they would not find a better meal than these three partially drowned Brontosauruses still unable to walk, still struggling to get their wobbly legs beneath their huge bodies. After losing their own breath in their attack, the Allosauruses themselves were not in best of health.

They approached like cats, each foot placed down softly. Still, their approach was seen by the sharp-eyed Pteranodons flying lower and lower to protect the recovering Brontosauruses. The fliers were sure that the three Allosauruses meant to eat the youngsters. They were stalking their prey, preparing to pounce. Their huge jaws were wide open, showing rows of sharp white teeth.

"Its the real thing," clacked Pteara.

"Their throats are big as tunnels," clacked Rono.

"And no light in the tunnels," said Don.

The Pteranodons were not smart, but they had good instincts. They knew they had to take action. At this point, Prince Albert, Princess Elizabeth and Baron Von Zack were all trying to help the young dinosaurs stand on their feet. Other plant eaters were nudging and lifting as best as they could.

Prince Albert had sent his Stegosaurus bodyguards to check the ravine where they had been attacked on their way to the slides. He

Water gushed from the youngsters' mouths.

wanted no problems on their way home. Prince Albert was very surprised when the Pteranodons flew low over his head wildly clacking: "Allosaurus attacking! Allosaurus attacking!" Albert had no time to plan a defense.

Then Pteara had a great idea. "Let's ram them with our beaks," clacked the wise old bird to her brothers. "We'll catch them by surprise."

"Ram them where?" cried Rono. "Their skin's too tough."

"Ram their throats. Their mouths are wide open." Without taking time to think the three Pteranodons came screeching down and rammed their beaks deep into the throats of the three Allosauruses. With a Pteranodon's beak stuck in its throat, each Allosaurus became very confused. Once more they could not breathe.

Growing weaker by the second, the meat eaters, with flying reptiles stuck in their throats, tried to escape. Meanwhile, most of the plant eaters stood still trying to get over such shocking events. Before they could decide what to do, Prince Albert and Baron Von Zack, using the same tail action they had used in the *Koo Koo Nut* game, banged their tails against the weakened Allosauruses' legs. Their feet flew high in the air and soon the Allosauruses were once again flat on the ground. They were all unconscious and each had a Pteranodon's beak stuck in its mouth.

Seeing the Allosauruses flattened out and appearing lifeless, all the plant eaters joined Prince Albert, Baron Von Zack and Princess Elizabeth in pulling the Pteranodons from the mouths of the meat eaters.

All of this required so little time that the Pteranodons,

Then Pteara had a great idea.

They rammed their beaks deep into
the throats of the Allosauruses.

once free of the meat eaters, could still half walk and half fly to safety. Meanwhile, all the plant eaters, including the youngsters with the wobbly legs, waded into the water to protect themselves from further attack.

If Prince Albert's bodyguards had been there they would have finished off Allo, Sorry and Rusty. Being very tough reptiles, the three Allosauruses soon were back on their feet. They looked toward the spot where they had intended to enjoy their evening meal of young Brontosauruses. The ground was bare. Looking beyond and into the lake, they saw that the plant eaters had formed a protective circle around the three recovering youngsters. Obviously, the Allosauruses' day was done. They would have to be satisfied with the Diplodocus' tail which at best was only an appetizer for three hungry meat eaters.

"We'll get them next time. It's a strange trail that has no turn," said a sad and beaten Big Al as he and his two brothers faded into the jungle.

The Homecoming

Chapter 21

Homecoming

After looking at the sun, Prince Albert said it was time they headed home.

"Mud slides can teach dinosaurs whether to go head first or tail first," said Albert as he quietly scolded the young dinosaurs for their behavior.

The Pteranodons also thought it was time they returned to the Great Inland Sea. They wanted to report to the Czar and Czarina what they had seen and done. The rulers of the Great Inland Sea had no idea about dinosaur life in the Carolina Blue Swamp Country.

"I suggest you spend one more night with us," said Prince Albert. "King Karig and Queen Violet will want to thank you for your courageous attack against the Allosauruses. Most likely they will want to honor you with a Royal decoration."

"That sounds nice," clacked Pteara, "but we really should be returning home. The Czzzar and Czzzarina will be worried. With our headlight fish bladders we think we can safely fly at night."

Rono then told Pteara they had forgotten their fish bladders at the cave. In their excitement to visit the mud slides, they had left their headlights lying on a rock near the cave. Pteara quickly agreed it would be smart to pick up their headlights since this might be the only way they could fly all night. In fact, those fish bladders just might change their lives by making it possible to fish at night. If Albert didn't mind, Pteara said they would fly to the cave, pick up their headlights, and, if the lights worked, fly all night to get home.

"Do what you must," said Albert, "but I hope you will still be at the cave when we get there."

King Karig and Queen Violet greeted the Pteranodons as they glided to a smooth landing at the cave's mouth. Pteara explained that Albert and his clan would soon be home. They were walking, of course.

"Yes, that's one thing we Brontosauruses cannot do," said King Karig. "We cannot fly."

Pteara replied, "But Brontosauruses can do other things well. For example, they protect their young." Before she could stop clacking about the brave Brontosauruses Pteara clacked out the entire story of the fight with the Allosauruses. And she told of their dive into the Allosauruses' mouths.

"That is the bravest act I've ever heard," said the old King. The Queen and I will issue a Royal decree. For this act you deserve our highest honor: The Order of the Magnolia Blossom."

Chapter 22

The Royal Ceremony

When Prince Albert and his clan arrived home, King Karig and Queen Violet were rigging the cave for a Royal ceremony. Grape vines loaded with bright blue grapes had been swung across the opening of the cave.

Prince Albert could see what was happening. The Pteranodons had told his parents about their savage battle with Allosauruses and the King intended to present some sort of honor. Prince Albert secretly hoped the Pteranodons would receive the Order of the Magnolia Blossom, the highest dinosaur honor, but it might be the Order of the Cherry Blossom or some other flower.

"Looks as if you're planning a Royal ceremony," said Prince Albert to his father.

"Yes, the Pteranodons have told us about the day's events," said King Karig. "We intend to bestow the Order of the Magnolia Blossom." Princess Elizabeth, Lady May and Lady Lynne became quite elated when they heard the news. This meant each Dinosaur's neck would be decorated for the event. The King and Queen would each wear a crown of green, brown, yellow and red leaves. The crowns looked like an upside down eagle's nest, but they fit the reptiles' heads comfortably.

Pteara explained to Albert that she was embarrassed to

cause so much trouble. She only wanted to tell the King and Queen of her admiration for the Brontosaurus, but the King had insisted on the ceremony.

"Don't give it a thought," said Prince Albert. "You and your brothers deserve our highest honor."

The King then asked the Pteranodons to line up in front of the cave. The Brontosauruses stood at attention under the grape vines, their noses high in the air. Baron Von Zack tried to bite a mouthful of grapes, but Elizabeth told him it was not proper during such an important ceremony.

"We eat grapes after the decree is read," said Elizabeth, "not during the ceremony."

Zack continued to look at the grapes.

King Karig asked Prince Albert to read the Royal Decree. In a deep voice Prince Albert read what his father had written. "On this day in 144 million years B.C. three Pteranodons from the Great Inland Sea, without any thought of the dangers involved, and in order to save the lives of three young Brontosauruses, did fly their beaks into the throats of three Allosauruses. Such action was above and beyond the call of duty. The King of the Brontosauruses hereby issues the Order of the Magnolia Blossoms to Pteara, Rono, and Don, and proclaims this day as Pteranodon Day. Signed, King Karig and Queen Violet.

The Pteranodons were touched. Their eyes moistened with tears. "This decree will be placed beside your signature at the Rock of Honor," said King Karig, "and you are welcome to bring friends to visit this Hall of Fame during your entire life."

Prince Albert read the Royal Decree.

Pteara said it might be nice to bring the Czzzar and Czzzarina at some future date. Perhaps the King and Czar could have a meeting.

"You may extend my invitation to the Czar for such a meeting," said King Karig. "Meanwhile, we know you have to be flying home. Speaking for all in this kingdom we wish you a safe journey, favorable winds, and a well-lit flight."

Queen Violet and Princess Elizabeth strapped the fish bladder headlights on the Pteranodons. The reptiles took off with enough light to make their night flight. They circled the cave three times, going higher each time, and then headed west.

Baron Von Zack told Prince Albert that he and the Merry Landers would spend a few days before returning home. Prince Albert said they would try the slides again. He doubted the meat eaters would show up for a long time and would search elsewhere for their meat.

Meanwhile the beaten meat eaters were passing the word not to go near the mud slides. There was danger of getting a Pteranodon's beak in one's throat.